Skin Again

Written by
bell hooks

Illustrated by
Chris Raschka

Jump at the Sun
Hyperion Books for Children
New York

Printed in Hong Kong

First Edition

1 3 5 7 9 10 8 6 4 2

This book is set in Lexicos.

Reinforced binding

Library of Congress Cataloging-in-Publication Data on file.

ISBN 0-7868-0825-X

Visit www.jumpatthesun.com

All the joy of the love community—to knowing
each other from the inside!
Lisa, Chris, Jackie, Anne, and Garen
—b.h.

For Mary and Nels
—C.R.

The
skin
I'm in

is just a
covering.
It cannot
tell my story.

The skin
I'm in

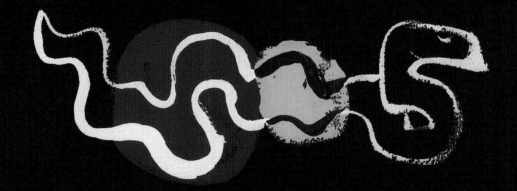

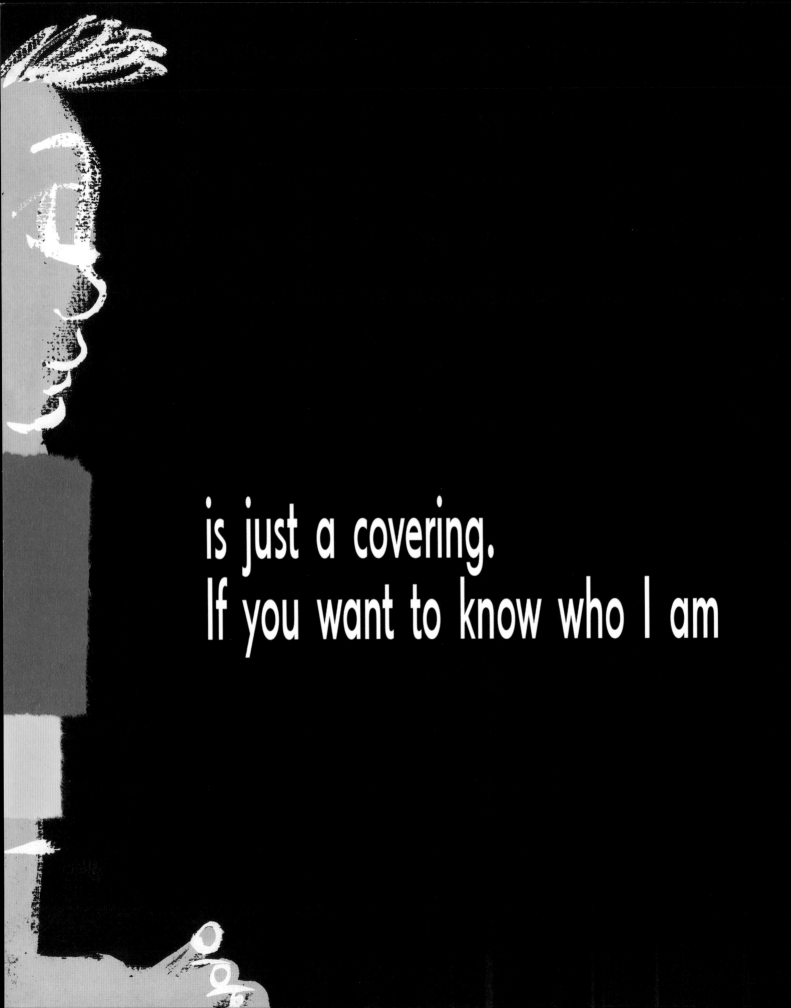

is just a covering.
If you want to know who I am

you have
got to
come
inside

and open
your heart
way
wide.

The skin
I'm in
looks good
to me.

It will let you
know one small
way to trace
my identity.

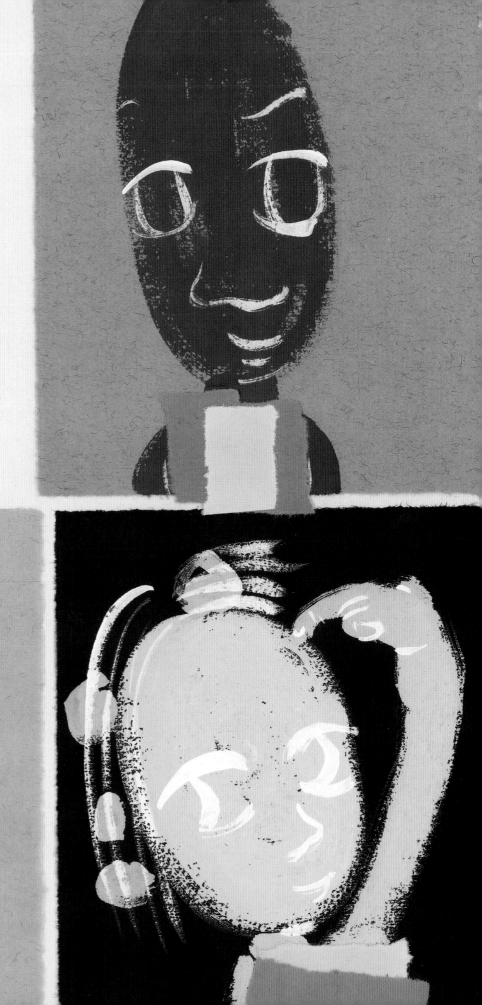

But
then
again

the skin I'm in will always be just a covering.

It cannot tell my story.

If you want to know who I am
you have got to come

inside.

Be with me inside the

me of me,

all made up

of stories present, past, future

some true to life

and others all

fun and fantasy,

all the way I imagine me.

You can find all about me—

coming close and letting go

of who you might think

I am

before you
come inside
and let me
be real

All real then. In that place where

skin again is one small way to see me

but not real enough

to be all

the me of me or the you of you.

For we are all inside

made up of real history,

real dreams,

and the
stuff of all
we hope for

when we
can be
all real

together
on the
inside.